Weather Report

The Heaventree Press
in association with
sampad

Weather Report

First edition 2005

ISBN 0-9548811-3-3

Graphic design by Bharat Patel, 2005

Heaventree logo designed by Panna Chauhan

Printed by
Cromwell Press
Trowbridge, BA14 0XB

Published by
The Heaventree Press
PO Box 3342
Coventry
CV1 5YB
England

Weather Report

Edited by
George Ttoouli

Published by
The Heaventree Press

in association with

sampad

Foreword

This publication is the culmination of a project that we began two years ago. This was one of the most interesting and evolving projects for us. An idea that was initially going to involve only local and regional participants – but became a global one.

The fact that responses to our idea, which came from young writers in the subcontinent, resonate with their peers in the UK, also proves the power of the internet. While the theme of 'weather' has a universal character, the writers here explore and respond to it with passion, candour and sometimes with a lot of humour, providing a glimpse into their individual world.

I hope this initiative will have provided encouragement to many young writers. Irrespective of the competition element in this project, it created an opportunity for creative expression for many young people, who impressed us immensely with the depth and quality of their thoughts and ability to communicate through words.

In sampad we believe in the power of the arts as a tool for change. We believe that it can bring individual creators together to become a force that cannot be ignored – breaking real and perceived barriers. *Weather Report,* I hope, will have achieved a united platform for sharing words and thoughts – a platform that will link young writers across borders and provide hours of fabulous reading for all of us.

Congratulations to every individual who has been involved in this initiative. This was important for us and you have helped us realise our dream. Thank you!

Piali Ray
Director
sampad

Contents

Acknowledgements

sampad would like to pass on their thanks to the following people who have helped to make this book possible:

Shefali Oza
The judges – Gurpreet Bhatti, Julie Boden, Daljit Nagra
Sukhi Jagpal
Anne Cockitt
The Heaventree Press
George Ttoouli
The British Council
Book Communications & Birmingham Book Festival
Orange Studio
Caroline Griffin
Everyone who entered the competition

sampad receives support from Arts Council West Midlands and Birmingham City Council

sampad is a dynamic South Asian arts organisation based in Birmingham, playing a significant role regionally and nationally in promoting the appreciation and practice of the arts originating from India, Pakistan, Bangladesh and Sri Lanka. The word sampad means wealth in Sanskrit and the organisation translates this as cultural wealth to be shared as widely as possible.

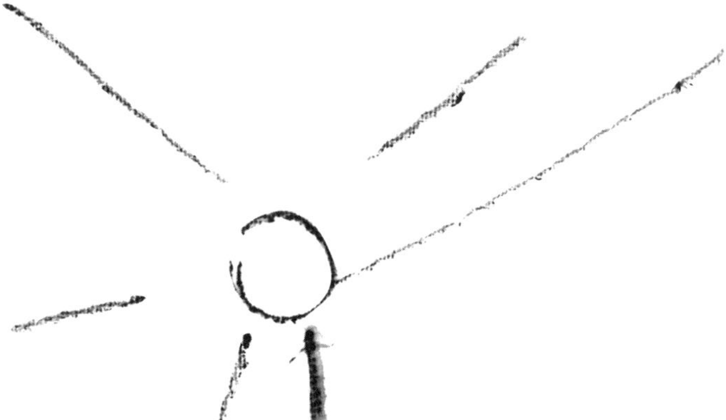

Winning Entries

Amrita Bandopadhyay, Kolkata, India

I am seventeen years old and a high school student from Calcutta, India. My interests include reading, writing and watching Hollywood classics. I also enjoy listening to music and travelling occasionally.

Various writers inspire me with their individual styles, like Jane Austen with her subtlety and wit and Thomas Hardy with his vivid descriptions of nature and fine portrayals of the complexities of human emotions and relationships.

I draw my inspiration from the ordinary people I meet every day. Nature inspires me in certain ways. The very act of writing also inspires me because I find creativity is one of the best ways through which I can communicate my thoughts.

Close to the Creator

Once it so happened that our trip to the seaside was cruelly interrupted by one of the heaviest downpours I had ever encountered. A while later the rain reduced to a drizzle leaving the garden of the hotel with a fresh rain-washed appearance. I decided to take a walk down the beach and slipping on a pair of sandals I walked out. On approaching the beach the scene I confronted left me spellbound.

It was twilight. At the end of the day the sun had made feeble efforts to peep out and somehow it had succeeded. Even as the sky was painted grey with irregular patches of white, a thin pale streak of gold tinged the sky. The sun seemed like a blob of orangeish yellow, not a majestic burning coin of copper. Even though the sky was not painted with the usual lurid twilight hues and a gloom loomed above us, there were still streaks of soft orange and pink giving the heavens a magnificent luminous glow.

The waves of the dark grey sea roared with all their might, vehemently protesting at the gloom above. The sand, muddy, was completely devoid of its pale, powdery glow. Only the phosphorescent grains sparkled.

As the sun disappeared below the horizon I stood drinking in the warmth of one of nature's majesties, with the wind lovingly caressing my face. As it got darker, I started to return, drunk with the smell of the salty sea, the sound of waves ringing in my ears.

Gioia Barnbrook, UK

I am thirteen and I go to Ninestiles Technology College in Acocks Green. My hobbies include listening to music, fencing, reading and acting.

The writer that has influenced me most is probably Jim Crace as his stories really come to life through his narration and you are left feeling like you have been to the places he describes. I feel he does exactly what a writer is meant to do; he tells brilliant stories that really take you somewhere else.

Eternal Nature

I could stand here forever,
Watching all over this vast landscape.
Looking out over a blanket of white,
Smothering the ground below.

I could sit here forever,
Watching shoots as they begin to rise,
Looking at the short, plain grass,
Dotted with plants beginning to grow.

I could lie here forever,
Watching the bees on their way,
Looking at the glaring sun above,
As it inspects its vibrant garden below.

I could sleep here forever,
Resting among the dead brown leaves,
Lying below trees stripped of their cover,
Preparing for the winter and snow.

I could stay here forever,
Watching the seasons roll past,
Letting the beauty of nature surround me,
I could stay here forever.

An Underground Home

The rain pounded on the dirt above me, an occasional drop falling through the gap between the wood and the ground above. By that time the hole was about four-foot-something, which meant I could sit in it. It was the only place where I knew I was safe, my hole, dug by my own hands. A safe paradise, where I could live all my life and no one would know. My safe, cosy hole, protecting me from the hardships of life, shielding me from the driving, stinging rain that had made my eyes and ears burn as I ran home. The black clouds above me were laughing, looking at me hiding, jumping whenever I heard thunder rumbling in the distance. They were taking immense pleasure in my fright.

I'd never liked rain, it makes me angry, especially when it feels like it's there just to ruin your day, just to make you personally feel miserable. I hate the thunder and lightning even more though, the way the lightning illuminates where it hits, the way thunder rumbles, like a thousand timpani players in an orchestra waiting for the final clash of cymbals.

Supreet Bhalla, UK

I am thirteen years old, and go to Lordswood Girls' School, Harborne. I am studying subjects including Maths, Englsh, Design Technology and I am doing some lunch time clubs such as cricket club. I am a librarian at school and I am doing my training at the moment.

My Grandad used to inspire me a lot but now he is no more in this world. He was a philosopher and a writer.

Narinder Dhami is a writer who has influenced me, I met her at mac. *My best friend encourages me a lot and means a lot to me.*

Thunder Night Full of Wonder

The sky was black
Covered by a huge cloud.
Wind blew, uprooting trees
Making noises very loud.

Many small clouds
Hovered all over the sky
Making it dull and gloomy
But the earth still was dry.

Deep cracks dominated the land
Dried by the strong sun
As the clouds refuse to rain
As if making fun.

The moon was hidden,
Showing only a small arc
Still the sky glittered
Though the night was dark.

Forbidden, still I crept out,
To view the mystic sight
Of the moon hiding behind a cloud,
But lending a bit of light.

The winds blew all over
Making a swishing sound,
As if whispering something
To the sun-baked ground.

I stood still, staring about
As if charmed, for the grace
Of the night was in trace.

Slowly the moon was
No longer hidden by the evil.
It came out and smiled
And its magic couldn't fail.

Then there was a bright flash
And clouds began to thunder,
Few drops fell on my face
And I looked around in wonder.

Rain fell heavily
Making me all wet
But I stood fascinated there
To see how earth and sky met.

I was totally soaked
Dripping from head to toe,
I skipped around the garden
Like a young doe.

I felt free and refreshed
And yearned to be out a little more
But the night was all gone
And the clock struck four.

I slipped inside and soon
Smuggled into the bed
And dreamt of drops of dew
On the sweet roses red.

This night of wonder
Is the one which will be
Never erased from my mind
And will always enchant me.

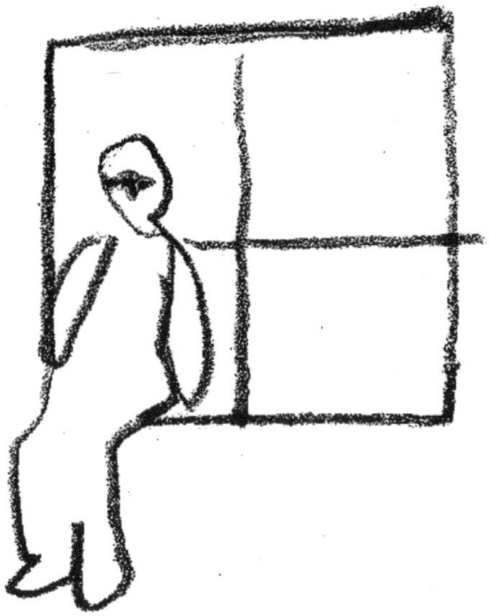

Arun Budhathoki, Nepal

I have just finished my 10+2 from Himalayan White House International College, in the Faculty of Humanities. My major and minor was English Literature and Journalism.

I spend my free time reading verses, listening to music, watching movies and worshipping nature. Nature inspires me to write, and human instinct too. When I am high or low or in any state I grab my pen and carve my reflection.

I am partly influenced by Keats, Wordsworth and Tennyson. My poetic spirit has drunk their songs, hymns, and muses. Modern poets like Dylan Thomas, Sylvia Plath and Ted Hughes have taught me that after living in an urban area I can't fully feel the trees, flowers and unpolluted rivers.

Another tear

I yelled for help,
So came the monsoon winds
And made me visible in my lake,
I looked around and smiled
Because of its darkness:
I let the leaf leave its slow poison in my lake,
I drank silently and calmly,
With small droplets of tears falling upon 'Good'
And I was making my waves burn:
Still, silent and soundless.

Black and White Cloud, Walking Alone

Force of sad winds
Erode plain image of a white cloud,
Walking alone binds
Lone walkers,

Huge body cover black cloud,
Within it droplets of soft fluid,
Dreamers wonder the giant's heartbeat,
Whisper lowly; friendship's seat
Combine two chariots,
They walk together,
When black cloud is sad: white cloud dissolves in pain,
When white cloud is jolly: black cloud disappears in bliss,
Walking alone, alone,
Alone walker share the eternal sky,
And am walking alone,
Alone,
There's no black or white cloud inside me,
Dot sky.

Changes

Cold dew, shouting to bright rays,
Saw me in warm clothes,
And released cold tone,
"You deceived me,
I hate you."
She packed her clothes,
And vanished for few days.
One fine morning,
Cold clothes, shouting to bright rays,
Saw her in warm garden,
And released cold tone,
"You cheated me,
I hate you."
Next year,
She was cold dew,
And I, 'warm cloth.'

Nonsense Sense

Breaking the top of frozen ice,
Slippery edge touches dumb water,
Cold and hot; hot and cold,
The mirror-crown shatters into bubbles,
Giggles inside blind liquid,
Edges touch bare skin,
Laughter in rotating wind,
Whirlwind, calmness, windy and soft breeze
Strikes crown far away beside farm of sanity,
The broken pieces climb over and over,
Over the last top, there reaches bubble and mirror,
A mystique mirror stolen from mystic person –
The Insomnia Fire.

Proposal

The cold rain smells not inner feeling,
But tingling words,
Falling softly upon cold dew,
The day leaf, in surprise,
Borrows green and tries to attract cold dew,
There is rain outside says dew:
I say, "Yes, I love you."

Rain

Black foam, white foam,
Flows beneath colourful sky,
Clasps, spreads above chosen place,
Chosen by the queen of heaven,

Secretly she's out of sight from Gods,
She changes her image into tiny droplets,
She falls without royal dresses, jewellery, beauty and fragrance,
She's fresh, sweet and nude,
She touches my every part,
I feel making songs of love for her,
She's the princess of earth,
She's mine. She's mine.
I'm still thirsty; do not make me dry,
O rain,
O princess of my heart.

Snowfall

Snowfall, snow in a cold place,
I sing for winter queen; smiles,
Smiling fire touches my face,
I dance with piano tune,
Sweet melody makes all asleep,
My heart, my baby is holding warm hands.

Cold-heart, cold winds in a slaughter place,
I hear fear, anger, and tears; blood-shed,
My elder son kills younger one,
'Help-Help!' daughter cries, as prying eyes
Rape her in a holy-shed,
My love, my husband is killed in a civil war.

Smoke opium; opium clear memories,
I forget beauties and sorrows; but can't forget myself,
The heartless clock mourns; it whispers,
"Tomorrow the child dies."

Gloomy is the night.
Voice penetrates firm mind –
"Gloomy Sunday;"
Raise hands with sudden surprise,
Break the source and dance for last tune,
In the midst of symphony, grab a knife:
Fire, clock, winter queen (no human voice)
Recall memoir, but vain:
Blood flows from child's neck,
Fall down, piano break.

Wind Forgotten

Slow movement of downward howling,
Pulls the upward tracks,
Feeling the sigh and shy of beauties,
Settles plain sheet on a windy place,
Moves the colourless leaf and falls into pieces,
The colour of sheet changes every moment
The voice of forest waves its speech,
It thanks for letting inside dark room,
And transforms the scene,
Slowly the speech is forgotten
As the vehicles and houses
And humans start to speak.

Sindhura Chakravarty, Kolkata, India

I am sixteen years old and am now in class eleven. I study in Loreto House, Calcutta. I like to read, write, listen to music and sing in the shower. I would like to think that blatant curiosity is not always bad.

I guess if anything inspires me to write it would be those instances in life that give us something to think about. It needn't necessarily be important, just something that makes you wonder, "What if..."

Different authors have influenced me at different times: The Little World of Don Camillo *by Giovanni Guareschi really moved me. It made me realise that one does not always need to be serious to be inspirational. Harper Lee's* To Kill a Mockingbird *is also a book that changed the way I perceive the world. I also enjoy reading Nick Hornby, Eoin Colfer and M.M. Kaye.*

A Hot Day in Kolkata

It was hot and humid, even for a summer's day in Kolkata. I lay sprawled out on the veranda, swatting sleepily at the odd fly with the newspaper I was too lazy to read, when something caught my eye.

There was someone in my neighbour's mango tree. Now if it was just another neighbour's shrivelled mangoes that were being plucked, I would not have given it a thought. The kids here are notorious for stripping any tree of the fruit of their choice, but for all their ingenuity they had not ever managed to get their grubby little hands on Mr. Sharadendu Banerjee's fruit.

Mr. Banerjee was a short, thin man of about fifty who was quick enough to teach any ten-year-old a lesson for having dared to come near his mangoes. His tree was famous for bearing the sweetest mangoes ever. Obviously I was interested to know which little monster had dared to pluck the forbidden fruit. As I looked closely at the half-hidden figure that had climbed the tree with such agility it reached out a long hairy hand to pluck a juicy, ripe mango. I started – that was no kid. The sudden jerk brought my rickety chair down with me in it. When I could look out again I only caught a glimpse of a small hairy creature jumping over the garden wall – mango in hand.

I shook my head in disbelief and picked up the fallen newspaper. The headlines read: Summer in Kolkata Zoo too Hot for Cool Chimp!

Dara El-Masri, Dhaka, Bangladesh

I am thirteen years old now and I come from Jordan. I am a student in Year Eight, going to be in Year Nine next year. This year I studied at Grace International School in Bangladesh. Now I am in Jordan and going to stay here and study in a new school.

I enjoy writing poems and stories about life. What inspires me to write is what is around, the problems I face and how I feel towards different types of things in my life. Adeline Yen Mah is my favourite writer, I like the way she writes and the words she uses.

I Am a Tree

I am a tree
always prepared for every season
I soak up the warmth of the sun
which smiles down at me

I stand
graceful to the wind
strong after the storm
cleansed as the skies cry,
mounting powerful, unnoticed.

I hang firm and steady
through the cold harsh winter
I am renewed at the first symbol of spring,
stay deeply rooted
while stretching for the towering sky

I study in Year Twelve in St. James' High School, Kolkata. I find that I have a knack for expressing myself through my writing and I would like to nurture this skill of mine.

I love writing short pieces on abstract topics and propagating my own little views of the issue. I also love listening to music and over the years I have built up quite a collection. Lately I have also developed a liking of photography. Here too, I cover abstract themes.

I'm a pretty introverted person and so I think I feel more comfortable laying down my thoughts on paper than verbally professing them. On the other hand, I guess I'm one of those people who like to let out their emotions, joys and strifes by penning something down.

Water of Life

The road ahead looked like a serpent, stretching on and on to eternity. On either side lay vast stretches of yellow sand – interspersed with rolling dunes and flat planes. That was all.

The sun was at its zenith and blazed down upon the world with its mighty rays, which seemed to strike the ground and, with each blow, take some of the life out of it. The road was cracked and the occasional solitary scorpion that came to the surface for a whiff of air, darted into the cracks as soon as it heard the approaching footfall.

Walking down the road in those thin-soled sandals was close to walking over red-hot coals. His feet were scorched black, his bare chest encased in layers of sweat. His eyelids were barely open, and looking into his eyes, one could see EXHAUSTION, personified. His dry, cracked lips were bleeding and blood was trickling down his chin and neck until it reached his shirt, sticking to his chest. His gait was bent and he was struggling against all odds just to keep himself going. His tongue groped about for that last drop which trickled down from his forehead, before it reached the ground.

Hope is something that is woven intricately in all parts of the human mind and it is this hope that kept him going. He saw before himself an angel. In her hand was that ever-elusive mirage, that tall glass, full of the Water of Life.

Carla Hadland, UK

I am fifteen years old and live in Droitwich Spa, Worcestershire.

Frogs in the Studio

STUDIO: And an unlikely trail of events followed a south Asian festival yesterday. The marriage of Muhammad Bhutan and Anita Rajah brought more than just wedding vows, after it started to rain – but not water! Tina West has the story.

REPORTER: Well, Ross, the marriage of Bhutan and Rajah was held behind me in this garden belonging to Bhutan's parents. When the couple had been pronounced married the singing and dancing commenced, and it started raining frogs. Now, the marriages in Asia are normally very bright and do have many events at the ceremony. It seemed the guests thought the raining of frogs was part of the actual show, but only realised it wasn't when the singers and dancers stopped. Now the experts who study rain patterns say that it is because of the heat wave in Southern Asia these past few days. It seems that when the water on the ground was being evaporated, it also picked up many of the small frogs out of the lakes. When it started to rain, it released the frogs. It is quite common, especially in the hotter countries. There have been reports of crabs, worms, fish, and even multicoloured stones in the past, spread across the world. The problem is so common here in Rutamahak, South Asia, that there is even a clean-up company specialising in putting small creatures back where they belong, after their fall from the skies. Needless to say, these companies are very popular! Tina West reporting for Central News.

SUBHI SYED HOSSAIN, DHAKA, BANGLADESH

I am fifteen years old. I am currently in the ninth grade in Scholastica School, Dhaka. I am to sit for my O-levels in May 2006.

I love sports, especially basketball. I love reading books and enjoy writing in my leisure time. I enjoy writing poems and short stories. I enjoy shopping, watching comedies on TV, eating out and chatting with friends. But nothing makes me happier than when I am playing.

My writings usually depend on my mood. I write just as it comes to me. Also the book I read before I write sometimes acts as an inspiration.

The writers who have really inspired me are Sydney Sheldon and J. K. Rowling. Each of them writes their stories with a twist in the tale. Their writing is very intriguing. I envied their style of writing and so I started to write myself, trying to organise my thoughts like theirs.

The Never-Ending Rain

Night fell as it started drizzling. I quickly closed all the windows. Although it was just drizzling, I could sense the unsightly black clouds in the growing night getting even more threatening. And just as I had predicted, after a few minutes a heavy shower of rain clattered on our rooftop along with the gushing wind thumping on our windows as if it was trying to knock down the glass into shattering tiny pieces. It was actually kind of scary. I was just glad that mother was at home with me.

Around eight p.m. mother and I sat down for dinner. Father was away on a business trip abroad.

Halfway through our meal the lights flickered and eventually they went off as a thunderstorm now raged outside. Mother told me to sit quietly as she called out to Farida, our housemaid, to light us a lantern. Farida came in a few seconds.

We finished dinner and I headed for my room to read a good book that would match the weather outside. I looked through my spooky collections and found a book called *The Never-Ending Rain*.

It did not exactly look my age but seemed like fun now, though when I was younger I was scared to read it, and so I thought I'd give it a try. Sprawled on the ground with a lantern beside, I began reading.

The story started off with a little town that was always very happy and did not want anymore, except for more rain, which only came once a year and so they had to work extra hard in harvesting their cornfields. The townsfolk were very merry and always stuck close together. But there was just one little girl at the far east of the town who lived with her rich parents and a beautiful sister. It looked like she lived the life everyone dreamed of but actually she was very unhappy. She was very smart and very kind but she was rather different looking than her family. She was actually rather unattractive and always wore strange dark clothes. Her family tried to persuade her into rich clothes or rather normal clothes but she refused.

Now her strange appearance clouded the minds of the townspeople who were little educated and thus believed in the curse that they had heard of from their forefathers. The curse as it was, had been put on the town, saying that a little unhappy girl would be born at the rising of the full moon at the end of the year, who would bring never-ending sorrow to the town. It also said that she would possess witchcraft, and thus curse the town once more. Now this little girl was born at a full moon around November and so it nagged the people even more in believing her to be the curse.

Often people would see this little girl talking to herself and throwing glances around at the other small girls of whom none were her playmates as they were all pretty much scared of her strange form, not to mention believed in her being the curse to their precious little town.

Little Aliya as she was named had always believed in supernatural powers. She had read many books relating to them and had loved every word of it. Thus she dressed like those who were of the 'dark age,' as she believed herself to be. Time and again she would wish that she possessed such powers that would curse the town that never spoke to her. Even her own family was ashamed to take her out with them. And thus she was usually left alone.

Years passed and suddenly the little ugly duckling transformed into a beautiful young swan.

Though young lady Aliya still wore cloaks, some people, especially the young boys, now actually talked to her, not coldly or with disgust like before, but with admiration.

That's when it hit her. "Judged by the covers did they?" thought young Aliya. "Well I'll teach them how to judge me!"

Meanwhile the annual rain had not fallen that year. Everyone was rather unhappy and the cheerfulness of the townsfolk ceased. Everywhere there was now dismay and thirst for the first drop of rain. As six more months passed it still didn't rain. People stayed inside the cool shades of their houses and prayed to God, for rain that was yet unanswering.

One day a meeting was held at the city hall where everyone was to be present. There they all consulted in what to do about the problem, but no one could come up with any solution. Just when they had given up hope Aliya raised her hand and told them that she could help them 'summon' the rain. And that was her biggest mistake.

Suddenly someone from the back yelled out that she was the curse put on the town, who had called for the rain to cease. He accused her of witchcraft and hatred towards the town, as they had never accepted her. Aliya was shocked yet outraged as she swore out loud, not really aware of what she was saying, that she would curse the town very soon, bringing sorrow that they could never imagine.

She burst out of the room and ran to a mango tree near a dry pond, where she collapsed and nine years of anger, sorrow and hatred poured out through fat drops of incessant tears. She did not know how long she had been there but she knew that her family did not care as she had disgraced their reputation. And so Aliya ran into the dry pond, sat in the middle and prayed very hard to God, her only friend, to bring such distress to the city that would never, ever end.

She cried on and on until suddenly tiny drops of cold water trickled on her bare feet. She looked up to see the clouds darkening and drizzles of rain all over town. She could hear the people shouting and laughing. It was deafening. She was very much shocked. She had thought that God was her only friend, but now He too had turned against her. She slowly dragged herself from the now very fast-filling up pond, and ran as fast as she could to nowhere. The storm raged over the town, yet she ran and ran and finally exhausted and hungry she came to a little hut and knocked on its door. A very kind old lady quickly opened it and let her inside. Aliya asked if she could stay the night and she was, by all means, welcomed by the lady. Aliya stayed for a few days, as the rain didn't seem to end. She only talked to the lady when necessary, otherwise kept to herself feeling strangely alone and upset as her best friend had now left her side.

Days passed but the rain never stopped. News reports around the country showed perfect sunny days in all the cities except theirs. The townsfolk were now getting very worried. And after some more weeks they were now very frightened.

And that's when Aliya knew that God was still her friend, the best friend one could ever have. That night she prayed endlessly to God for his gift to her and curse to the town.

Months passed and the rain never ended. People were now calling on relatives to shift homes and after a few more weeks the town had lost all its members except Aliya.

As the people moved out Aliya began a new life, all alone, somehow surviving by mere will power, and although the rain had now stopped, fields lay barren and houses flooded. The ex-members of the town heard that the rain had stopped; yet they never dared to go to the place as they knew that Aliya still lived, the cause of their downfall. But while some were still frightened and some hated her, others pitied her and regretted treating her the way they did before.

*

As the story ended it concluded that the very little town now had no occupants, though Aliya had passed away long ago, as anyone who went to live there still experienced the horrifying life of a never-ending rain.

The storm still thrashed outside and closing my book I thought to myself that I had heard of a town like that before... hadn't I? Or was I just too engrossed in the story. Well, as I dozed off, I prayed to God that the rain would stop when I woke up.

Saeed M Hussain , UK

Being of dual heritage it's always been difficult to 'fit in' until I realised, why not celebrate this fact and explore my own culture through my writing! Currently I am just an ordinary college student undergoing my A-Levels, with the aim of studying English Literature at a top-class university.

However one day I hope to be an international phenomenon and won't rest until this has been achieved! I've always been inspired by everything in life, but my grandparents, Samera Jabbar and the one and only AG, have been the divine revelations that I have needed to make all my work possible, be it for advice, companionship or everlasting conversations about the trivial things in life!

It's Raining Chaat and Dahl!

"It's Raining Chaat and Dahl!" My mother used to say
When Aunty went into the kitchen on a cloudy day.
Knives against countertops and spoons around the pans.
A hurricane was quieter than the sound of the extraction fans!

The sorcerer of saag, the conjurer of chutney.
Ninety-nine different names for Aunty who worked abruptly.

Aunty's sheer power smashed the four-minute mile.
As she kneaded the dough typically desi style.
Yet perfection were the roti that she made.
This from the woman that killed her first husband
with a garden spade!

Thunder would roar and lightning flash,
But Aunty continued even though sweat dripped from her tash!

Tremendous she was, stupendous she is.
When it comes to making meals Aunty's the biz!

Her samosas are always piping, refreshing is her tea.
I can't tell you how much I love Aunty-ji!

She'll put on a show and always will heavily load the table.
This is why from behind she looks like she belongs in a stable!

But as the weather settles and the puddles dry up.
You wont get no more chaay, not even a second cup!
As Aunty believes that you should eat whenever it rains plenty.
This is her excuse for moving to England where you always
get drenching!

Sunita

Sometimes the clouds mask you as if they are your veil
Other times you are there uncovered, naked for all to see.
You glow so bright, have rosy cheeks, never are you pale.
But you are always there and ever-loving, the giver of life to me.

You shine and shimmer as if you are a spark that will never cease.
Your flaming locks constantly flow, I imagine to your knees.
How old are you Sunita?
When were you born?
I often wonder what you would reply.
Are you married?
Do you have kids?
Can I be your guy?

I don't know what I've done to deserve your presence.
But I can't imagine us apart.
When you send down those warm waves I feel them directly
in my heart.

It appears to me you always use haldi
as your hands are forever snow.
Yet at times I see you throw in chilli
as the crimson waves make you bellow.
Your food must be instantly made
as your tandoor is constantly roaring.
From such a height and your access to the world,
the food I eat must look miniscule and boring!

It kills me to say this my jaan but married we can never be,
Because my beloved Sunita you are 93 million miles away from me!

The Four Seasons Terrace

Winter sat at the head of the table,
Giving everyone a frosty glare.
Snow had covered his head top,
Making brilliant white of his hair.

Spring had now approached and plopped herself right down.
Glistening was her face that opposed Winter's glum frown.
Sun shone from her eyes and life bloomed from her lips.
This sense of new beginnings went right down to her hips.

Summer are the parents always in a fluster.
Overheating about bills that are clenched up in a cluster.
Yet they are always calm, emitting rays of joy at night.
Despite they are in debt and in a constant state of fright.

Autumn keeps them all united, a go-between some would say.
He is a model son, even though Indian and gay!
Controversial he is, sheds away all sense of strife.
But he knows when to go away and allow the beginning of life.

See if we look at them right now, happy they may all seem.
As this close-knitted family at the table will artificially beam.
Yet no matter which one: Winter, Spring, Summer or Fall.
At time to time they'd just love to crawl up in an inaccessible ball.

But how can we judge in this diverse and plentiful land?
When instead of disputes we should all lend a helping hand.
We should look at this Asian family as the perfect example.
As no matter what label they have, be it old, gay or stressed,
They have an ensemble.

Nayeem Islam, Dhaka, Bangladesh

I come from the biggest delta in the planet, Bangladesh. I am a 9th Grade student of the Aga Khan School, Dhaka. My interests lie in programming, graphics and animation, while I also spend a good amount of my time in reading storybooks.

I think the injustice, violence and emotional changes around me inspire me to write, to express my views and opinions. Writing also allows me to express my feelings and emotions, which have been very valuable to me during my teens. Anita Desai, Jules Verne, Mildred D. Taylor, and Anna Sewell have influenced me because of their innovative storytelling methods and the way in which they voice their opinions through a brilliant plot, always maintaining simplicity in their language.

The Captive

The clear sky finally gave away to a drizzling downpour. The colour blue flickers against my weak eyesight as drops of rainwater navigate down my cheeks to give me its taste. I didn't want to go away to a dry place this time I wanted the rain to saturate me with emotions that no longer exist in me.

The rustling raindrops take me to a life beyond where I perhaps had a heart that knew how to cry. I can remember there was once a time when my mother kissed me on the cheeks and all roads in life led to dreams. When my little sister played with her doll. She was afraid of the dark but the lustrous darkness had taken her away from me. And I don't see her smile anymore that motivated all my dreams. The persons close by me have all become inanimate and it is difficult to find my shadow beside me.

Someone has plunged a dagger into my heart for it no longer pumps life into me. I no longer smell the lilacs, daffodils and roses that bloom in Regent Park for the exuberance of youth has abandoned me. The sun no longer illuminates my dreams, I try to break the sadistic cage that imprisons me but I remain trapped in a dungeon of machines. The rain has stopped, yes, it's my tear trickling down my cheeks and the colour blue no longer flickers and I become as silent as the graves that neighboured my melancholy.

Taaeba Khan, UK

My age, as I write, is eighteen. I am currently studying my final year of A-levels to include the subjects Philosophy, History, English Literature, Islamic Studies and Critical Thinking.

When I am not studying, I am teaching at an independent grammar school. For recreation I like to tend to my garden and observe the growth of my variety of exotic plants and flowers. I also enjoy reading and writing poetry. My greatest influence is the great eastern philosopher, Rumi.

Storm

Lightning struck at quarter-to-nine
As she put her neck on the line
I need room to breathe
She began to plead
And it flashed again
So bright
There was going to be a storm tonight

Room to breathe, what for?
We give you freedom and you want more
This isn't what you were brought up for
He yelled as the rain began to pour
Her parents were prepared for a fight
There was going to be a storm tonight

I'm not like you, she pointed out
We agree, they began to shout
You're more fortunate, more lucky
You have so much opportunity
They were going to prove themselves right
There was going to be a storm tonight.

I know I'm blessed

And I'm grateful
But come down to my level
I want to find my own fortune
She explained
Inviting a monsoon
She tried hard to disguise her fright
There was going to be a storm tonight

We only want what's best for you
One day you'll understand
And as outside rose a deluge
She announced: I've found myself a man
His name is Simon
He's white
There was going to be a storm tonight

Please say that's a lie
Why, beti, why?
How could you bring such shame on us
And destroy our trust?
The banks shattered with immense might
There was going to be a storm tonight

Water levels began to rise
Drowning out her resonant cries
You aren't to see him anymore
We're catching the first plane to Lahore
Our worlds don't mix
They collide
There was going to be a storm tonight

The tempest arrived and left again
Sweeping her away before daybreak
Her parents tossing and turning
Unaware but awake

The past, present and future
Failed to unite
There was a brutal storm last night

Water
Written in response to the tsunami

Water left me standing
I'd call myself invincible
But I have no home
I'd call myself invincible
But I'm all alone

Water came and annihilated
All that dared stand in his way
Water came and eradicated
And then retreated again

Water created this wasteland
A mass of carcasses;
I knew their names
Water created these walking corpses too
Astounded. Staggering. Assessing their fate

Water left me thirsty
Ironic, I know
Water left me drowning
In this torrent of sorrow

Water left me standing
I'd call myself invincible
But I have no home
I'd call myself invincible
But I'm all alone

Alone but Dignified

She'd spent her entire lifetime under the blazing sun, and so laughed when I tried to describe snow to her.

"I'll have to see it to believe it," she had told me, shaking her old head.

"You will, inshaAllah," I had whispered, more to myself than to her.

I was eight then. Almost ten years from now, we'd sat together on the parched ground in the North West Frontier. I was on holiday, but for her it was just another day. Another long and hot day, spent in anticipation of the rain.

"What's living here like?" I'd asked her. I'd seen so many films about village life. It looked like fun. They worked hard, but then broke into song every now and again; a reflex in response to the music that would come out of nowhere.

But this wasn't a movie from Bollywood or Lollywood. It was reality. There was no Shahrukh Khan or Dilip Kumar in her world. Born in an isolated village, a twenty minute walk from the Khyber Pass, she'd grown up labouring on the wheat fields. Her children had all grown up, and had flown the nest. They'd flown all the way to England, and wrote occasionally.

"I can't read," she told me, with tears in her eyes. She'd wipe them away as quick as they'd arrived, and smile at me before carrying on with her work. She was lonely, but she'd never let go of her dignity.

"I don't want to be dependant on anyone," she told me, when I'd asked her what she wanted most in life. "And I want to see this snow thing you're going on about."

She died in Selly Oak Hospital last week. Cancer, the doctor had told us. But I knew better. It was the loneliness that had killed her.

It had been snowing that night. I hope she saw it.

Pranawa Koirala, Nepal

I have just finished my Twelfth Grade and currently I am in search of universities for furthur studies. I have a variety of interests, like painting, music and martial arts, apart from writing.

Being from a middle class family in an underdeveloped country, I live in a society full of biases. I have seen families where people die of obesity, while the families next door die from malnutritoin. Such a disparity in this beautiful country provokes endless feelings in me and, as William Wordsworth once said, "Poetry originates from emotions recollected in tranquility;" these feelings in me when they are triggered emerge in the form of poems.

Of all the poets whose poems I have read, chewed and digested, William Wordsworth takes the credit for most sustainable effects in me. I love the poem in which he expresses the kinship between nature and the soul of humanity and how we humans are moving far apart from nature.

Bonded Hearts and the Rainy Key

When life's pool dries up
due to torrid heat,
of the monotonous race
to make one's life a feat,
nature sprinkles its holy water
to revive the dry pools,
to arouse the fragrance of soil it cools
from the blissful stream,
then through my bonded mind
peeps a childhood dream...

Quenches thirst of the dry soil,
whets new hopes in the seeds,
and whispers through fragranced breeze
tales of its noble deeds.
From far and beyond, from the desert sands,
to the blessed lives and those blessed lands.

How the people thanked, sang and danced,
how they wetted themselves in those wetted lands.
Then through my jealous brain,
creeps and peeps a childhood dream...

Man is now none but a puppet,
in his own hands,
shackled by his own rationale
and always driven to advance,
looks at the joy of winning the race,
overlooks the joy he every moment misses
so near yet so far are we,
from those moments we don't see,
from the freedom of bonded hearts,
and the heavens' gifts of glee...

So, when life's pool dries up
and nature sprinkles its holy waters
in the form of rain, give me courage
to revive my dreams in tatters,
to break the shackles, to break the chain,
to end the race, to end the bargain
of my heart with mundane gains,
and a childhood dream peeps through all these pains,
to live every moment, down to a grain,
to be free and dance in the rain.

Anila Majid, UK

I am twelve years old. I am a pupil at Lordswood Girls' School in Harborne, where I am studying English, Maths, Science, History, Geography, Music, Citizenship and Art. My hobbies are reading and writing. I also like researching the lives of interesting people.

The enjoyment I get from reading well-written and entertaining stories makes me want to write, too. I have been much influenced by Narinder Dharni. Jacqueline Wilson and Roald Dahl, as these writers write very funny stories and understand how children think and feel.

In the Wind Tunnel

Several summers ago my parents, my brother and I were on holiday in the town of Murree in Pakistan. Murree is a large, very busy town in hilly country.

On our first day in Murree we left our hotel and went into the bustling town centre to do some shopping. The sky was bright, but overcast, and the wind was strong.

Our shopping done, we started to make our way back to the hotel. By this time the wind was angry. It was howling and blowing at gale force, an experience that made us feel like ants in a wind tunnel exposed to the whine and blast of a huge fan. To make headway against the wind we had to lean into it to avoid being blown over and to use great will – and muscle power. Eyes and noses were shielded as rushing grains of sand stung our faces and plastic litter swirled past us.

Unfamiliar to the town and disoriented by our struggle with the wind, we asked for help to find our way back to the hotel. Luckily we were soon given the directions we needed. For most of the way the wind remained stubbornly hostile, making progress slow and frustrating.

It was with sighs of relief that we finally re-entered our hotel after our encounter with the fury of the wind. My brothers and I decided that we would rather *not* be ants in a wind tunnel!

Anu Manthri, UK

I am seventeen years old and I am currently in the sixth form at Queen Mary's High School. I study English Language, English Literature, History and Biology. Aside from school and work I sing and also write.

One of my favourites has to be The God of Small Things *by Arundhati Roy, but it isn't easy selecting favourites because everything is different and it's good to have a varied selection of reading as opposed to one or two set topics or types.*

My Observatory

Sultry monsoon air passive and warm in my nostrils and mouth; each breath tasted on every taste bud – magical tastes of the Indian city.

At the top of my Nani-ji's house there is a room much like a tower-top prison. Looking down on to the muddy orange street I can see a lot – a small monkey, its brown fur dishevelled in the sheets of clinging rain. Hurrying into a shelter it starts to spruce its freshly washed maniacal hairdo.

Cars drive past revving their struggling engines, skidding and stopping frequently to avoid the pools that were simply puddles a few hours ago. Whooooosh! A fountain of water rises and falls from where the tires hit a lake-sized puddle.

The eastern archway is the tower's darkest bearing, where shadows creep over deserted roads and packed little homes and the monkey battles with its Mohican. Looking west where the protagonist sun clings hopelessly to the sky as he is captured by darkness, to remain prisoner.

The fiery determined sun breaking and bleeding crimson in to the heavens. The few remaining flickers of scarlet trickle away like blood oozing from a wound.

The monkey is asleep and the shadow of the guava tree has run away with the spoon.

The rain softens as though it too is answering the sleepy call of the night and tiny warm droplets of heaven shape silver angels against the black, where I watch from, at the top of the house – in my observatory.

Ahel Maswood, Kolkata, India

I am currently studying in the Sixth Standard in St. James' School, Calcutta, India. I love writing poetry, playing the piano and dancing to rock & roll. Reading is another hobby of mine.

I write for my complete pleasure.

Walter Dean Myers, the author of Somewhere in the Darkness, *is one author who has inspired me to write. I admire his way of portraying touching human relationships. Rabindranath Tagore is another author and poet I admire. I love his beautiful poetic relation to Nature.*

Spring

The beautiful word 'spring' beckons me to go outside,
The bird tells me, (on its back) to take a ride,
Travelling through the air, I see the sun melting the snow
And see the fresh flowers and leaves grow.
Free from the world of winter at last,
Over everyone's head a gloom it had cast,
But now I'm in the world of spring,
Where everyone rejoices, and the birds only sing.
In no mood for studies, I sit in the classroom,
While outside, the birds watch everything bloom.

The beautiful word 'spring' is music to my ears,
Winter bids goodbye, sorrowfully shedding tears.
A riot of colours wipes out the dull black and white,
The blue and black pens are filled with colours bright,
But from these pens, flow, neither History nor Maths,
all that comes to my head is poetry,
Spring inspires you to write and write more, no one wonders
how easy it could be!

But in the end, poetry or Maths, it's all the same, with the
only difference to set them apart,
One, I write with my hand, the other I write with my heart.

Deena Mehjabeen, Dhaka, Bangladesh

I am thirteen years old, turning fourteen this July. I am studying at The British School in Year Eight. During my free time, I love reading books. Sometimes I also listen to music.

Whenever a thought comes to me, and I feel like writing on it, then I just do it. Besides that, my whole family and my school teachers encourage me, so they are the ones who always inspire me to write. I truly appreciate the books of Jacqueline Wilson and she has influenced me the most through her writings. I love every word she uses to portray each character and their feelings. She writes as if the characters are in front of her and we cannot really say it's all fiction.

Weather

Summer brings warmth, light and happiness for many.
But for us, lots of Kalbaisakhi's storms.
Children gather unripe mangos
That drop like hail as storms rage on for long hours.
The tin roofs of houses are
Blown away as winds roar and lightening strikes
As the tempest calms down,
The fear of facing the
Re-formed village arises.
Shall we go and see whose tree
Fell on whose fence?

Gabriela Moskalova, Dhaka, Bangladesh

I'm thirteen years old, I was born on 7th October 1991 in Czech Republic. I live in Bangladesh with my parents right now. My dad is a dentist and my mom is a nurse. I like playing tennis, playing soccer and swimming. I go Grace International School, Dhaka.

That's probably everything about me.

I Wish

I was on the beach one day.
It was raining.
I waited for someone to come and look for me.
No one came.

The wind was blowing hard.
I felt cold.
Every few minutes a car passed by
but not even one stopped, to pick me up
and take me home.

Everything's so twisted, so strange.
I feel alone.
No one cares that I'm gone.
The wind is still blowing,
It's really cold.

I wish someone would come
  and take me home.

Claire Ormsby, UK

I'm seventeen years old and I'm in the sixth form at Rugby High School for Girls studying English Literature, Drama, Biology and Latin, as well as a GCSE in Ancient Greek. I love to read and write and I spend time online where I collaborate my writing with the writing of others from around the world.

I write because I have a story I want to share. I get ideas and sometimes I want to see where they will take me, or how my characters will react to them. It's experimentation, like cooking – what happens if I add a bit of this or that?

My influences: J.K. Rowling, because of the way she carries a story, Gail Carson Levine because her characters are so appealing and William Goldman because of his witty narrative. Also, the people I've worked with online who have worked personally with me to help me improve and my friends, Hannah and Emily, who I've written with since I was eleven and who keep encouraging me all the time.

Typical British Weather

Sometimes it rained heavily. Sometimes it thundered in a very impressive way. Sometimes it misted in a way that made hair frizz and sometimes it drizzled in a rather depressing manner.

Sometimes it rained in sheets and sometimes it rained in blankets. It very rarely rained in quilts, but that was another matter entirely.

Sometimes it rained in torrents. Sometimes it just rained.

Today, it was raining in clouds. It was as though the Rain simply couldn't be bothered and was just sprinkling out a little bit of moisture because it felt obliged to. The Wind was trying to help, but wasn't making a very good job of it and the result was what was essentially a very soggy breeze.

The Sun wasn't impressed with the Rain's lazy attitude to work, but as the Rain had been picking up the slack left when the Sun decided to halve its hours in order to pursue a correspondence course in Philosophy, it couldn't really complain if the Rain was feeling a little run down after its enthusiastic displays over the summer.

The Snow was keeping out of it, trying to wake up the Frost, which was stubbornly insisting that it had plenty of time left and could easily sleep for a couple more months before it was needed. The Snow couldn't understand why the Frost acted like this, as though it hated work. The Snow loved its job and faced it with exuberance whenever it was required.

Just typical, eccentric, British weather.

Purnima Pendurthi, UK

I am known as 'Nimi' and I was born in 1993, in Birmingham. Both my grandparents came to England in the 1960s from Andhra Pradesh, in South India, to work as doctors in the NHS.

My favourite subjects are English, Science and Art. I attend Priory School in Edgbaston, in Year Seven.

Travel, especially within Andhra Pradesh, is what inspires me to write. India arouses all the human senses in many distinctive ways. All the elders in my family love to read, and have encouraged me to do so, particularly Indian writers in English: Anita Desai for her evocative imagery and R. K. Narayan for his narrative. Both writers conjure up witty descriptions of people.

Mourning for the Monsoon

The sky darkened suddenly. Purnima reached for her shawl, which she had draped over the veranda charpoy. She sighed. He'd been gone for two months, now, and had promised he'd come for her birthday on the twelfth of July. The monsoon threatened to make a dramatic appearance. Now the monsoon was late, and so was her father.

He had left on his usual, last-minute business trip which should have ended by July twelfth – her birthday, it was too late now, and weeks had gone by.

Her feelings had come in stages. At first, she had felt sorry for herself; then, towards the monsoon, she had felt angry and neglected. Now, the heat boiled in her veins, as she thought of her father enjoying the cool, American autumn.

Earlier that day, she had watched other children play with their fathers, outside in the pre-monsoon fever. She had thought of her birthday, when friends had boasted of gadgets, gifts from America. Now she only felt the oppressive monsoon clouds bearing down on her. She glanced up at the now swirling, metallic clouds and, fearing a cloudburst very soon, picked up the bamboo chair cushions and went inside.

Every afternoon after school Purnima's so called friends boasted about how their parents came for their birthday and brought them the latest gadgets from America. So every day they boasted, and every day Purnima ran away and cried herself to sleep. That night the hot moist winds blew up all the dust on the veranda of Purnima's house. Through dinner, her mother asked her why she was so quiet. Purnima merely shrugged. Inside, the servants were squabbling, beating the floors with hand-held bamboo sticks.

The air was moist, stifling; the moon was hidden behind a thick blanket of cloud. After dinner, as usual, Purnima ran up to the veranda and talked to the moon like a diary. Purnima, whose name meant, 'full moon,' begged it, with tears swallowed back.

Then, as if from nowhere, Purnima's mother was at her side, her right arm around her and, in her left – a letter. She recognised at once the small, neat letters of her father's handwriting. Inside, the date – the fifteenth of August "...coming in two weeks' time... the first of September..." TODAY! As Purnima wept and danced, she felt the hot rain, like tears of joy from the moon. She danced and danced, as the balmy rain saturated her hair and her satin salwaar kameeze.

Georgina Phillips, UK

I have recently finished studying for my GCSEs at Bromsgrove School. In my spare time I am a keen athlete, running for the county. I also enjoy being creative, my favourite subjects being Art and English.

I was first inspired to write when my teacher lent me the book My Left Foot, *by Christy Brown. I was amazed at his determination to express himself and be recognised as an individual and how he finally managed to type books having control only of the toe on his left foot. Surely if someone went to so much effort to express themselves, those of us who take our health for granted should try and do the same.*

My English teacher Mrs Farr got me interested in poetry, the hours that our class spent studying poetry made me realise just how much can be expressed both directly and indirectly in a poem, in a way no other art can do.

When Sun met Rain

Sun was a little girl I knew a few years back
With fiery hair and dark brown eyes, she stood out from
  the pack
Sun was the most beautiful girl you could ever hope to meet.
When anyone saw her, their hearts always skipped a beat
She wore a dress that flowed so long and far, it flew above
  the ground
And when anyone touched it, happiness was found
Sun filled all people, friends or foes
With that feeling of pleasure, that everyone deserves to know

But Sun had an enemy
Rain, who had an awful tendency
Of making others feel, sad, dull and upset
Yet when, these enemies met
It was not a battle that took place
Instead they stood, glared and looked each other in the face
And they always realised that they were quite alike
Despite their differences, Sun was not one to cause a fight

As Sun's dark brown eyes glared at Rain's blue
They realised that they needed each other, to solve the clue
Together they made magic and colour flew from their eyes
Suddenly Rainbow appeared, causing a huge surprise
Whenever Sun and Rain decided to stay away
It always resulted in an incomplete day
So Sun and Rain often meet together, to bring all true delight
Since Rainbow brings such pleasure along with Sun's light.

SATVEER PNAISER, UK

I am eighteen and am currently studying at King Edward VI High School for Girls, doing Latin, French and English Literature A-levels. My A-levels have exposed me to varieties of literature. Latin and French literatures often revolve around philosophical debate, immorality and passion, giving rise to my own desire to explore and understand humanity.

I have been inspired by Thomas Hardy on many levels. His work evokes a tragic perspective. I admire his exquisite and powerful poetic ability and find his work truly transcendent.

Other writers who I admire purely for their skill in reaching out to the reader are L.P Hartley, Sylvia Plath and Elizabeth Strout. I love reading and believe it is an important requisite for the next generation for personal and spiritual growth.

Powdered Rain

But if you stared long enough at the rain that fell so secretly that it could hardly be seen, you saw a hidden place, a place that until now you had only ever been able to feel with your heart.

This was how she stared now. Outside the grass was full and drenched, already saturated, but the rain continued to fall, unheeding and soft, like the lowering of eyelashes, impossible to resist. Her stomach began to rise and fall at the bittersweet scene, remembering and yearning.

She wanted to push the past back, far from her mind, but the air had her now, it would have been easier to send the rain back up to Heaven. As if to taunt her, the water began to rush down harder. The sound of it made her eyes dart sidewards as if surprised, as if she had provoked the skies, only for them to have left her breathless. When had she wished for more? More anguish, more pain, if she had wished for it then it was delirium, an intoxicating suffering that equated to her existence.

A voice came shouting through her thoughts, calling her away. She glanced at the puddles now forming on the grass as she closed the door, the water and earth separating, never to remain as one. She walked away and allowed a prayer to escape that he had been watching it too.

Tabassum Rasheed, UK

I am fifteen in August and in Year Ten at Stratford-upon-Avon Grammar school for Girls. My chosen subjects for GCSE are History, Geography, Latin, and Drama, but I enjoy all my subjects. My hobbies include singing, dancing and acting and I also enjoy lessons in Bharatanatyam, a classical South Indian danceform.

I like writing because it's an easy, calming way of expressing yourself. The unique thing about reading literature is that everybody sees and interprets it in different ways. Words have such a wide variety of meaning and I think it is great that no one can read the same thing the same way.

I get inspired by everything. If it fires off ideas in my head, I usually do something with them. Many writers have influenced me, mainly fantasy writers, such as Philip Pullman and JRR Tolkien. I'm also influenced by mythology from ancient cultures. Old stories and tales are fascinating.

Fortunes Under a Cloudless Sky

Red tiles glow in the afternoon sun,
Their age apparent by their blackened surface;
Perched at the edges – crows.
Sleek, black, they are omnipresent here.
Their repeated caws ignored by those who have
Lived with them for so long its absence is more noticeable;
Only heard by the foreigners and the tourists,
Or the occasional appreciative listener.

Such a one now listens, her face turned up to the heavens,
Rays of sunshine from a cloudless sky beating down on her.
Falling beams that illuminate the depth of her pencilled eyes
And throw fluttering shadows on the ground behind.
She sighs almost inaudibly, then stands;
The chimes of her anklet adding to the cacophony around her,
Breathing out with the sigh the last of her dreams.

Cloudless sunlit sky changes to cloudless moonlit sky,
The crows are silent, their scavenging for the day over.
Prevalent now are the voices of the night – the chirps of crickets
Broken by the barks of restless dogs and the cries of the drunk.
The clear night is a blessing to the desperate thief;
His pride breaking down in the face of his young child's cries,
Determined to provide in some way for his flesh and blood.
Offering a quick prayer to the gods while prising apart the roof tiles.

Cloudless sky again is host to the dawn.
The intertwined colours shining down on the fortunes of those
Sleeping under the shadow of the seven hills.

Naadia Saleem, UK

I am fourteen years of age. I attend Bishop Milner Catholic School in Dudley; I have recently taken my SATs examinations and am currently studying for my GCSEs next year. I enjoy reading, playing sports and one day hope to become a successful writer.

The work I've produced at school and at home, has been inspired by everyday life, by different situations people are put through and sometimes I let my imagination wander! Writers who have helped to influence my style of writing and genre are: JK Rowling, Sophie Kinsella, Garth Nix and Tess Gerritsen.

The Beauty of Nature

As your tears flow down one by one,
The rain patters on the ground.
As your eyes meet mine, you shy away
The sun hides behind the clouds.
I would pull down the stars for you,
You mean so much to me.
Darkness still remains in my world,
   If only we could make it be…

When you smile your cheeks blush rosy red,
The sunset glows over the sea.
You brush your hands through your hair
The wind blows so swiftly.
The love we shared was incomparable,
Yet love blinded you, you didn't see
If only you would realise,
   How much we are meant to be…

As you raise your voice,
The thunder begins to roar,
As you clamp your hands to your face
The blue sky can't be seen anymore.

No matter what a day I've had,
You are my sunshine, through the rain
Though my heart may keep on longing,
    You are the remedy for my pain.

When you used to smile at me,
The sun would shine so bright.
When you grew tired and fell asleep
You twinkled like a star, at night.
But you really are my shining star,
You were always there but far away.
Lighting up my world at night,
    But you could not be seen in the day.

KIRAN SAMRA, UK

I am sixteen years old. I am currently studying at Lordswood Girls' School in Year Eleven. I have a fond interest in Science and aspire to go on to study Medicine. I enjoy reading pre-1914 literature like Jane Eyre *and* To Kill a Mockingbird, *as well as books like George Orwell's* 1984. *I am also fond of Alfred Lord Tennyson's poem, 'The Eagle' and 'Patrolling Barnegat' by Walt Whitman.*

There are many cultural poems which I feel I can connect with, one of which is Sujata Bhatt's 'Search For My Tongue'. At times I also feel like I have been distanced from my Indian culture, but, like Sujata Bhatt, I realise that I can never lose my culture because it is part of my identity.

My life and the people around me inspire me in my poetry. I have written poems about every significant person in my life. My feelings, emotions and worries provide the basis for my poetry.

I Feel

I feel like what I see,
Loneliness clouds over me.
Raindrops drizzle down my cheek,
My mind is all foggy and so bleak.

I feel like what I see,
Excitement shines through me.
My eyes glow with glee,
I cannot escape this overwhelming heat.

I feel like what I see,
Confusion blows past me.
Wind pulls at my hair to compete,
As I whisper my very last plea.

Romer Sandhu, UK

I'm fourteen years old. Right now I'm at school doing my GCSEs; my favourite subjects are History, English and French. In my spare time, I do kickboxing and like hanging out with my mates.

My ambition of becoming a successful journalist is what inspires me to write and the poet Sylvia Plath has influenced me in my writing massively because of her sometimes controversial yet emotive poetry.

The weather according to me...

Weather *n tempestas, aer, aeriser.*
1. A determiner of one's mood. *The rain put a dampener on my spirits.*
2. Different forms of weather include rain, sun, slate, hail, snow [climate conditions].
3. A meteorologist. One who predicts changes in climate see meteorology.
4. A state of atmosphere; conditional to variables such as velocity, moisture etc.
5. Feeling under the *weather* informal. A state of bad health.
6. As a result of the rain and sun intercepting one another *formation of a rainbow is possible* [An arc of spectral colours]. *An illusionary hope.* Chasing the rainbow in hope of finding an answer. This could lead to a pot of gold and is likely to brighten up one's day.

Shahmuddin Siddiky, Dhaka, Bangladesh

I am a student of the Aga Khan School, Dhaka, Bangladesh. For my A-Level courses, I am studying Economics, Law and Pure Mathematics – all of which I really love. Apart from these, I am also involved in intra- and inter-mural debating, public speaking, community services, peer coaching and, of course, writing.

I cannot recall a time when I did not want to become a writer. Even as a toddler, I doodled out my own version of Thomas the Tank Engine. *Although writing is a difficult life, there are many I am truly grateful to for their unfaltering support – my parents and all the English teachers I have come across.*

There are also thousands of authors, including Toni Morrison, Stephen King and John Steinbeck, who have written novels for me to read before bedtime – every single word inspired me.

Danger... Brainwashed Human Beings Ahead

Many believe that the next century will be dominated by robots and sophisticated gadgets taking over human beings. Hmmm... interesting. Yet, little do we, Homo Sapiens, realize that we are already being controlled – programmed, commanded, monopolised – by something monumental. I mean, not like the robot stereotypes – all gray and steel, with funny sounds of static. The real culprit is something more cunning. It is a shape-shifter. It is a colour-shifter. It is...

The Weather.

Yes, it is the seemingly innocent cycle of rain, sun and clouds that is eating our lives, feeding on our freedom. By now, you must be wondering how something so mundane as the weather can substitute the laser-throwing, out-of-the-world gismos...

Well, think of how weather affects our day-to-day decisions. A day when the sun smiles and its rays cascade down prods us out of home – you know, to play baseball, sunbathe. On the other hand, a day with heavy downpour and charcoal clouds locks us home.

Worse, the weather is the master of emotional politics. It can bring us joy, or dump on us misery.

Did you notice how many people the weather kills every year? How about the headlines reading "Storm Causes Plane Crash" or "Twister Kills 12"? You revolt, you die. It's that simple.

Evil robots are fantasies, but the totalitarian weather is reality. It is an endless Holocast, an Orwellian nightmare. Terrifying… but believe it!

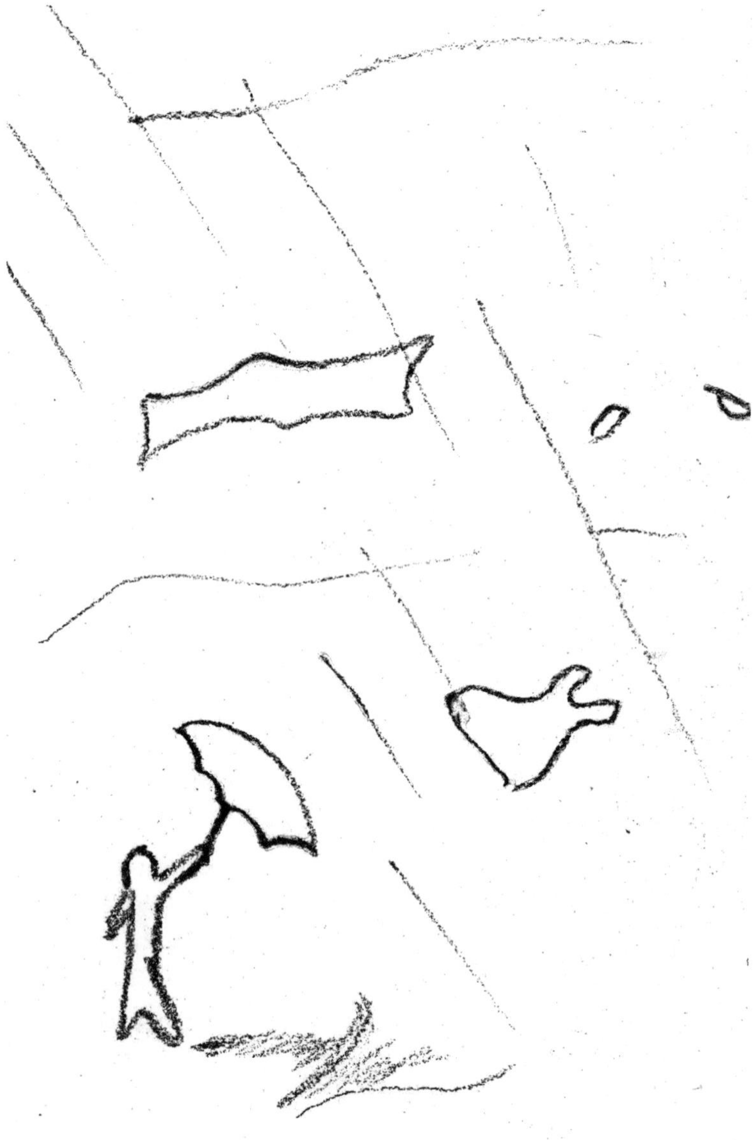